SUMMER CAMP CRITTER JITTERS

written by **Jory John**   illustrated by **Liz Climo**

Dial Books
for Young Readers

Whoa.
Why are you in
a tree? Shouldn't
you be, like,
down here?

Well, yes,
ha ha, as it happens,
it's my first year as a
counselor. I wanted to
make a good impression,
so I made this banner,
and then I got stuck,
so... I may just have to
be your counselor from
up here this summer.
Any questions?